ILLUMINATION
PRESENTS
SING

Adapted by
ARIE KAPLAN
Based on the film *Sing*

Illustrated by
ELSA CHANG

A GOLDEN BOOK • NEW YORK

Sing © 2021 Universal City Studios [...]
Published in the United States by Golden Books, an imprint of Random Hou[...] [...]use LLC,
1745 Broadway, New York, NY 10019, and in Canada by Penguin Random H[...] [...]en Book,
A Little Golden Book, the G colophon, and the distinctive gold spine a[...] [...]LC.
rhcbooks.com[...]
Educators and librarians, for a variety of teaching too[...]
ISBN 978-0-593-12140-5 (trade) — ISBN [...]
Printed in the United States of America
10 9 8 7 6 5 4 3 2 1

Buster Moon owned a theater. He put on shows where performers sang and danced. Everything looked so glamorous! But audiences stopped coming to the theater.

Buster thought of a way to bring in the crowds.

"I'll give them a show they cannot resist," he told his friends **Eddie** and **Miss Crawly**. He would have a singing competition!

To do this, Buster had to hold auditions.
Many animals tried out for the competition,
but four worked the hardest—

Rosita
the pig,

Johnny
the gorilla,

Ash the porcupine,

and **Meena** the elephant!

They loved music so much!

Buster chose the singers he wanted in his show.
"Get some sleep, and dream big dreams," he told them.
Things didn't work out perfectly during rehearsals.
Meena was too shy to sing.

"This stage is set to explode with major **PIGGY POWER!**"

And Rosita had a hard time with her
new dance partner, **Gunter**.

Some of the other contestants had troubles, too.

Johnny was upset because his father, **Big Daddy**, a bank robber, was in prison. Johnny missed him.

The biggest problem of all was that Buster owed money to the bank. If he didn't pay the bank soon, it would close the theater!

Buster convinced a legendary opera singer, **Nana Noodleman**, to attend a rehearsal for the show. If she liked it, she would give him money to pay the bank!

At first, the rehearsal looked wonderful! Buster had filled a
water tank with squids. The squids created a dazzling display
of color and light!

Nana was amazed.

But then the water tank burst open,

and the theater was flooded!

Soon the entire building collapsed!
WHOOOOSH!

Buster was sad. He quit the theater business and decided to wash cars . . .

. . . with his fluffy koala body.

But he wasn't alone. Eddie and Miss Crawly helped him.

Then one day, the contestants from the canceled competition visited Buster. They felt bad because he had lost his theater. They decided to hold the singing competition in the space where the theater used to be!
Everyone pitched in to build scenery and set up.

Soon the big night arrived. The audience was small at first, but Rosita and Gunter were a hit! They had finally learned to cooperate as a team.

Many more audience members arrived. They loved Rosita and Gunter, too.

Before long, the theater was packed.

Even Johnny's dad showed up!
"I'm so proud of you, son!"

When it was Meena's turn to sing, she remembered what Buster had told her: "Don't let fear stop you from doing the thing you love!" This helped her overcome her nervousness—and she brought down the house!

That was when Buster noticed someone very
special in the audience. It was Nana Noodleman!

Nana paid the money that Buster owed to the bank. Buster had a theater again!

And the contestants had a place where they could always perform. Now they weren't just Buster's contestants. They were his friends.